Horse and Pony Basics

Marion Curry

GARETH**STEVENS**
GS PUBLISHING
A Member of the WRC Media Family of Companies

Please visit our Web site at: www.garethstevens.com
For a free color catalog describing Gareth Stevens Publishing's list of
high-quality books and multimedia programs, call 1-800-542-2595 (USA)
or 1-800-387-3178 (Canada). Gareth Stevens Publishing's fax: (414) 332-3567.

Library of Congress Cataloging-in-Publication Data
Curry, Marion, 1954-
    Horse and pony basics / by Marion Curry. — North American ed.
        p. cm. — (Horses and ponies)
    Includes bibliographical references and index.
    ISBN-10: 0-8368-6831-5 — ISBN-13: 978-0-8368-6831-9 (lib. bdg.)
    1. Horses—Juvenile literature. 2. Ponies—Juvenile literature. I. Title.
  SF302.C86   2007
  636.1—dc22   2006002854

This North American edition first published in 2007 by
Gareth Stevens Publishing
A Member of the WRC Media Family of Companies
330 West Olive Street, Suite 100
Milwaukee, WI 53212 USA

Gareth Stevens managing editor: Valerie J. Weber
Gareth Stevens editor: Leifa Butrick
Gareth Stevens art director: Tammy West
Gareth Stevens designer: Kami M. Strunsee
Gareth Stevens production: Jessica Morris and Robert L. Kraus

Picture credits: Cover: Miles Kelly Archives; p. 6, 12 (top) Shires Equestrian products;
p. 16 (bottom) Jenny Deakin; p. 18 Lisa Clayden; p. 19 Janice Boyd. All other images
from Miles Kelly Archives, Corel, digitalvision, DigitalSTOCK, and PhotoDisc.

Printed in the United States of America

1 2 3 4 5 6 7 8 9 10 09 08 07 06

★ *Cover Caption* ★
Horses are herd animals and like company.

Table of Contents

Words that appear in the glossary are printed in
boldface type the first time they appear in the text.

★ Fossils show that the earliest **ancestor** of the horse was about the size of a small dog. This early horse lived in North America 55 million years ago. It is called *Eohippus* or the "Dawn Horse." Eohippus had short legs, four padded toes on its front feet, and three toes on its back feet. It probably lived in the forest.

★ These animals were **nomadic**, roaming in herds for safety. They traveled great distances to find food. Over millions of years, they changed, developing long legs to move quickly and escape enemies. Their toes changed into hooves. Over time, these early horses became all the different horses of today, including zebras, mules, and donkeys.

> The differences in size and shape of the horses below show how the animal has changed over millions of years to fit new conditions.

Eohippus   *Mesohippus*   *Parahippus*

- The early horses developed differently in different climates. Horses that lived in hot climates grew fine hair that allowed heat to escape from their bodies. Horses that lived in cold areas grew thick coats to keep them warm.

- More than 150 distinct breeds of horse and pony now live on Earth.

- Tribes from Mongolia in eastern Asia were the first to **domesticate** horses about five thousand years ago. People kept the animals for their meat and milk and also used them for transportation.

- For centuries, horses have served people on farms, in industry, in warfare, and in sports.

> *Pliohippus* had a longer neck for **grazing** than earlier kinds of horses. *Equus* had longer legs for running faster.

Merychippus   *Pliohippus*   *Equus*

Body Talk

* A horse's normal temperature is 99.5 to 101.3 °Fahrenheit (37.5 to 38.5 °Celsius).

* A person can tell when a horse is cold by touching it behind its ears.

* Horses do not need blankets if their coat has not been clipped. A horse will grow a long, thick coat to keep warm naturally in winter. Clipped horses need blankets to keep their **flanks** warm.

* A horse can see a moving object clearly, but it has trouble telling the distance between objects.

* Horses see some colors, such as blues and yellows, but not all the colors that most humans see.

A horse blanket should fit snugly around the neck and yet allow for plenty of shoulder movement.

* A fast **gallop** is a horse's best way to escape danger. It often sleeps standing up so it is ready to run. When a horse sleeps, its leg joints lock together. Keeping its legs stiff prevents it from falling over.

★ On the average, a horse has drowsy periods that last between two and four hours a day.

★ An ergot (also called a chestnut) is a hard growth behind a horse's **fetlock**.

★ *Fascinating Fact* ★

Horses enjoy oranges, grapefruit, and dates in warm countries where these fruits grow.

Horses **groom** each other and will often try to groom the person who brushes them.

★ Horses' eyes are set far apart on either side of their heads. This position allows them to see in almost every direction at once — except directly in front of their noses and directly behind their tails.

> This horse appears relaxed. Its ears show no sign of fear or anger.

★ Horses have a more highly developed sense of smell than humans. Horses are able to recognize their human and animal friends by smell alone. Horses are also sensitive to scents in their environment, such as that of dung, dirty water pails, moldy feed, and certain plants.

★ The whiskers that grow from a horse's muzzle and around its eyes are used like an insect's antennae. The horse uses them to feel nearby objects. Never remove these whiskers.

> Most horses have dark-colored eyes. This horse has a blue eye, called a walleye. Most horses with walleyes have one blue eye and one normal eye.

★ A horse's ears indicate how it is feeling. If a horse flattens back its ears, it may be feeling angry or scared.

★ Touch is one of a horse's most developed senses. A horse can sense a fly landing on any part of its body and use its tail to flick it off. A horse responds to touch all over its body, especially on its ears and eyes.

★ Horses have large ears that can move around and point toward sounds. Each ear can turn halfway around.

Most horses have four natural **gaits**: walk, **trot, canter,** and gallop. This **mare** and **foal** canter across a field.

★ Markings are areas of white hair on a horse's body. Some markings have particular names, such as *star* or *blaze*. Markings help people identify animals.

★ A snip is a small area of white hair above the horse's top lip or around its mouth.

★ Horses have feathers — clumps of hair growing behind their fetlocks. Some breeds have very fine, short hair. Others, such as Shire horses, are famous for their long, thick feathers.

★ White socks that extend above the knee are called stockings.

★ Ermine marks are dark spots on top of markings just above a hoof.

★ Some white hair growths are not natural markings. They are the result of old injuries.

The names of the white leg markings refer to the different points on a horse's legs.

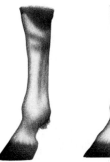  

Over-knee   Mid-cannon   Fetlock

Half-pastern   Crown   Coronet

Snip

Star

Stripe

Blaze

White face

Different patterns of face markings help identify individual horses.

★ Chestnut horses vary from reddish brown to deep reddish gold.

★ All-white horses are called grays.

★ A palomino has a pale gold coat with a light mane and tail.

★ The coats of piebald horses have black and white patches. Skewbald horses' coats have brown and white patches.

★ Strawberry roan and blue roan describe a reddish brown, brown, or black coat speckled with white or gray hairs.

★ A dark bay horse is brown with a dark mane and tail. A light bay has a lighter-colored coat and dark mane and tail.

★ Spotted horses have gray coats spotted with black or brown.

Horseshoes

- ★ People have protected horses' feet with shoes for more than two thousand years.

- ★ European horsemen started nailing metal shoes to horses' hooves around the sixth century. By the sixteenth century, heating horseshoes at the **forge** before shoeing the horse was common.

- ★ Not all horseshoes are nailed on. Sometimes, plastic shoes can be glued on.

Every horse owner should have a hoof pick for cleaning horses' feet.

The pointed end of the **anvil** allows the **farrier** to shape a shoe to the correct size.

- ★ Racehorses wear special lightweight shoes made of aluminum instead of the typical iron shoe. These shoes are called racing plates.
- ★ Special **studs** are sometimes added to shoes so the horse's feet can grip icy ground.
- ★ Someone must clean out a horse's feet twice a day to make sure no mud, stones, or sticks are trapped under its shoes. These items could make the horse **lame**.

- ★ The term *farrier* once meant "horse doctor" but now refers to a person who shoes horses.
- ★ Farriers are highly skilled. They understand how horses move and how to make and put on shoes. They also understand foot diseases.
- ★ Farriers can fit a shoe onto a horse at the forge. They can also take a light, compact forge to clients' stables and fit horseshoes there.
- ★ Today, farriers must have a lot of training to qualify as professional farriers.

After removing an old set of shoes, farriers must trim the horse's hooves before putting on a new shoe. They must make sure the horse's feet are even.

Herds

★ Horses are very social animals. In the wild, they prefer to live in family groups. These groups join together into herds.

★ A herd is usually led by a mare. She decides when the group should move on to look for fresh grazing.

★ One **stallion** in the herd will always be on guard. If he senses danger, he will alert the others who will follow the lead mare.

In a herd, horses who get along well with each other will groom and nuzzle each other. They also graze together.

A lead mare keeps the herd calm in foggy weather.

★ Horses are able to run very quickly, reaching speeds of up to 30 miles (48 kilometers) per hour in four seconds or less. They cannot gallop for long periods of time, however.

★ In the wild, foals usually stay close to their mothers. When there is danger, the adults move the foals to the center of the group to protect them.

★ Horses use their body movements and sounds to signal other members of the herd.

★ Horses rarely fight or try to injure one another. They show anger in other ways — by lashing their tails, flattening their ears, or striking out with their front legs.

★ Horses on farms or ranches often feel unsafe if no other horses are nearby. It is important to offer a horse some company — if not another horse, then a donkey or sheep.

★ When a horse is sold or dies, leaving another horse alone, the remaining animal will often miss its friend and appear sad.

★ Fascinating Fact ★
In the wild, horses spend up to 70 percent of their time grazing.

Foals

The Shetland **pony** foal will grow a thick mane and tail like its mother to protect it from the rain and the cold.

★ When foals are born, their legs are almost as long as they will be when they are fully grown. Newborn foals cannot eat grass because their long legs prevent them from reaching it.

★ Most foals are born in the spring. As the weather warms up, mares will find the best grass of the year to eat.

★ Foals can see well almost as soon as they are born. Within an hour, they can stand up and walk.

★ Within a day, a foal can gallop to keep up with its mother.

A young foal has very long legs compared to the rest of its body. As it grows, its body gets bigger to match its legs.

- ★ A newborn foal will often kick if anyone other than its mother touches its **hindquarters**.

- ★ Foals tend to sleep flat on the ground rather than standing up.

- ★ Foals like to play. They enjoy chasing and grooming each other. In the wild, **fillies** may stay with their mothers for several years as part of a family group.

- ★ Foals cut their first teeth within a week and have a full set of teeth by nine months.

- ★ Foals start eating solid food — picking at grass or digging in their mothers' feed buckets — when they are six weeks old.

- ★ A male foal is called a colt. A foal is called a yearling after its first birthday. Horses are fully grown by the time they are three or four years old.

A mare will continue to give her foal milk until it is about six months old. By this time, the foal will be eating other foods and can leave its mother.

* Horses enjoy being able to pick at food over a long period of time.

* Horses enjoy doing the same thing every day. They like to eat at regular times and stay near familiar companions.

* Horses like taking the same roads every day. They may not want to ride out alone if they are used to riding with other horses.

* Horses love company, especially other horses.

* Horses like baths if the weather is really hot. Sponging them or hosing them down cools them off.

* Rolling on the ground after exercise is fun for a horse.

* Horses enjoy having the freedom to graze and to roam where they want.

Horses enjoy rolling. It is good for their blood flow and skin.

Good grazing gives horses a choice of grasses and herbs.
Horses are fussy eaters and will not eat weeds such as thistles.

★ Most horses enjoy scratching themselves against trees or walls. They sometimes even try to rub against people.

★ Horses usually prefer to be stroked instead of patted.

★ Horses who get along will groom each other and nibble the skin at the base of the withers — the ridge between the shoulder bones of a horse.

Horse Dislikes

★ Horses hate to be tied up so tightly that they cannot move their heads or look around.

★ Horses hate to be chased by people or animals.

★ A horse may kick anyone who approaches quickly from behind. Any unexpected event may scare a horse and make it run or buck.

★ Horses dislike riders who pull on their mouths and are unbalanced in the **saddle**.

★ A badly fitting saddle or **bridle** will make a horse unhappy. All horse harnesses should be comfortable.

★ Mares become unhappy if separated from their foals. They will cry out for them if the young animals are missing.

★ Horses will become bored if left in a stable for a long time. They may start behaving badly — smashing stall walls, tipping over feeders — to show how they feel.

★ Horses do not enjoy nonstop rain. If their coats become soaked through, they may develop skin sores. This condition is called rain scald.

★ A stone caught in a horse's foot can cause pain. If small stones or sharp twigs tear the sole of the hoof, the foot may become

> ★ Fascinating Fact ★
> Many horses are afraid of pigs.

20

infected, and the horse will have trouble walking.

★ Horses have good memories. A horse will often remember a place where something scared it. Thunder or any other loud noise can frighten a horse.

A horse's first reaction to danger is to run away. With its ears laid back, this horse shows signs of fear.

It may always act nervous and be hard to handle when it returns to that spot.

Horses in War

* Horses were important in war because of their speed and **agility**. Soldiers on horseback had many advantages in battle over foot soldiers. Horses could also carry messages and goods quickly over long distances.

* The Roman **cavalry** was made up of foreign soldiers on horses who fought for Rome for pay.

* In 330 B.C., Alexander the Great's horsemen chased an enemy king more than 400 miles (640 km) in only eleven days.

* The **stirrup** was invented in the eighth century. It made a rider steadier when a horse was moving. A steady rider could use weapons more effectively.

* Ulysses S. Grant, Civil War general and president of the United States, loved horses and owned many. His favorite horse was Cincinnati. He only let two other people ever ride him.

* To North American Plains Indians, horses were very valuable, and tribes fought over them. When the Nez Perce Indians lost several battles with the U.S. cavalry in 1877, their fine Appaloosa horses were almost wiped out.

* The British military used one-half million horses in France during World War I from 1911 to 1918.

Horses and riders wore armor during battles in the **Middle Ages.** The armor was heavy and slowed the horse down, but it protected the animal.

★ World War I was the last time horses were used on the battlefield. Horses could not cope with **barbed wire**, modern guns, or the soldiers' deep **trenches**. About 6 million horses went to war. One million of these came from the United States. Only a tiny number returned home.

★ Germans used the Trakehner horse from Prussia as a riding horse in wartime and as a workhorse in peacetime. During World War II from 1939 to 1945, the breed was nearly wiped out when Russia invaded Germany. Horse breeders tried to take their horses to safety. Hundreds of horses died.

★ During World War II, the British army used the Dartmoor area in England for training soldiers. The number of Dartmoor ponies dropped rapidly. Now their numbers are increasing.

23

* Before the 400s, farmers used oxen rather than horses to pull carts.

* When formal grass lawns became popular in England in the eighteenth century, grazing animals and workers with hand tools kept the grass short. The first mowing machine to cut grass was invented in the 1800s. Horses pulled it, wearing leather boots to avoid hurting the grass.

* After the Industrial Revolution, from 1750 to 1830, horses carried goods into towns. They performed many jobs — from carrying coffins at funerals to pulling garbage carts.

* Horse-drawn mail **coaches** began running during the late eighteenth and early nineteenth centuries.

* People often overworked or beat their horses. Richard Martin campaigned in England for better treatment of horses in the early 1820s. In 1824, a group of people in England started the Society for the Prevention of Cruelty to Animals (SPCA). They closely watched the conduct of coach drivers and other people who worked with horses. The organization became a model for many others around the world. The first American SPCA was founded in 1866 in New York.

* From April 1860 to October 1861, riders for the Pony Express carried mail from

St. Joseph, Missouri, to Sacramento, California, a distance of 1,966 miles (3,150 km). The riders rode Mustang and Morgan horses. They changed horses every 10 to 15 miles (16 to 24 km) and changed riders every 75 to 100 miles (120 to 160 km). The trip took only ten days.

★ Horses pulled the first streetcars. In 1832, New York was the first city to have horse-drawn streetcars.

★ Horses also pulled narrow boats along the **canal** systems in the United States and Europe. These horses were called barge horses. They walked along the tow paths beside the canals.

★ The mining industry in Britain used **pit ponies** to haul coal and other minerals from the mine. In 1913, there were seventy thousand pit ponies. Some mines still used ponies as late as the 1990s.

★ People used horses in all areas of farming and transportation for hundreds of years. When machines were invented, trains, tractors, cars, buses, trucks, and electric streetcars replaced horses.

★ The word *horsepower* still describes the pulling power of an engine. One horsepower is equal to 745 watts or the work a horse can do in one minute.

Machinery drawn by horses, such as this seed drill, made farming easier and faster.

Movies and television make cowboys' lives seem more exciting than they really were. Cowboys moved large herds of cattle through the prairies.

★ A cowboy's most prized possession was his saddle. Even if he gambled away everything else, including his horse, he would keep his saddle and carry it on his back.

★ The Plains Indians put a brand on their horses to show which horses belonged to which tribe. Their horses were the **descendants** of horses brought to the New World by the Spanish.

★ Horses were important to North American Indians because they allowed the Indians to move faster and transport goods more easily. Indians used horses for war and for hunting.

★ The North American Indians believed that some patterns on their colored horses stood for magical properties that would protect them in battle. The Shoshone Indians hung special objects around their horses' necks.

- The Sioux Indians painted horses on their tepees and made halters and ropes out of horsehair and buffalo hide.

- The Crow Indians were famous for their horse skills. They were excellent riders and knew just how to talk to horses.

- Annie Oakley, Buffalo Bill, Butch Cassidy, Sundance Kid, Calamity Jane, Jesse James, Wild Bill Hickok, and Wyatt Earp are some of the famous cowboys and cowgirls in United States history.

- Gauchos of Argentina in South America are like North American cowboys. People say that if a gaucho is without a horse, he is without legs.

- The completion of the telegraph in 1861 put the Pony Express out of business. Stage coaches continued to carry mail, but the telegraph delivered messages faster than horses.

★ *Fascinating Fact* ★

Indian warriors painted their horses with designs meant to protect them and give them courage. Hand prints, stripes, or animal designs were popular.

Cowboys wore chaps over their pants to protect their legs while riding. These leggings could be made from goat, bear, or sheep skins.

27

* A famous story says the world will end when the four horsemen of the **Apocalypse** appear. The horsemen represent the four evils of the world. Conquest rides a white horse, Famine a black one, War a red one, and Plague a pale-colored horse.

* Pegasus, the winged horse in Greek **mythology**, carried Zeus's thunderbolt. He was born from the blood of Medusa, who had snakes for hair.

* In Norse mythology, Odin, the god of war, had an eight-legged horse called Sleipnir. He could gallop faster than any other horse and travel across the sky and the sea.

* The unicorn is a mythical beast that has the body of a pure white horse

According to legends, the horn of the unicorn could make poisonous plants burst and die.

★ Kelpies appear in Scottish mythology. These creatures live near running water. They make people get into deep water by appearing as beautiful humans. Then the kelpies drag the people underwater and take on the form of water horses.

and a single twisted horn on its head. The unicorn stands for goodness and purity.

★ According to Arabian stories, Allah created the Arab horse "out of a handful of the southern wind."

★ In Irish mythology, the horse carries the souls of the dead from this world to the next.

★ Poseidon, the Greek god of the sea, rode a **chariot** drawn by fantastic creatures that were half horse and half fish.

★ In Greek mythology, the gods of the sun and moon rode chariots across the sky each morning and evening.

Centaurs are imaginary creatures that are half man and half horse. They had the head and upper body of a man attached to the back and legs of a horse.

29

Glossary

agility: ability to move and turn quickly

ancestor: an animal or person from whom an individual or group is descended

anvil: an iron block for shaping metal

Apocalypse: the end of the world

barbed wire: twisted strands of wire with sharp points

bridle: a horse's headgear that includes the bit and the reins

canal: an artificial body of water

canter: a quick run with a three-beat rhythm; slower than a gallop

cavalry: soldiers on horseback

chariot: a two-wheeled battle car

coaches: four-wheeled carriages

descendants: over a long period of time, the young of an individual or group

domesticate: to teach an animal to live with humans instead of in the wild

farrier: a person who shoes horses

fetlock: a tuft of hair on the back of a horse's leg near its ankle

fillies: young female horses

flanks: the fleshy side of an animal, between the ribs and the hip

foal: a baby horse

forge: a workshop with a furnace

gaits: ways of moving on foot

gallop: a fast run

grazing: feeding on plants and grass

groom: to clean a coat

hindquarters: the hind pair of legs of a horse or other four-legged animal

lame: unable to walk without pain

mare: an adult female horse

Middle Ages: period of time from the fifth to the fifteenth century

mythology: body of stories that explain beliefs

nomadic: moving from place to place without a fixed home

pit ponies: ponies that were used in the mines to turn wheels or pull carts

pony: a small horse, less than 14.2 hands high (57 inches)

saddle: a rider's leather-covered seat

stallion: an adult male horse

stirrup: a pair of small rings attached to the saddle for a rider's feet

studs: nails with large heads

trenches: deep ditches

trot: a moderately fast walk

For More Information

Books

Everything Horse: What Kids Really Want to Know about Horses.   Kids Faqs (series).
   Marty Crisp (NorthWord)

A Field Full of Horses. Read and Wonder (series). Peter Hansard (Candlewick Press)

Horse Sense. Pet's Point of View (series). Beth Gruber (Compass Point Books)

Why Do Horses Neigh? Puffin Easy-to-Read: Level 3 (series). Joan Holub
   (Dial Books for Young Readers)

Web Sites

Kids Domain — Horses Links
www.kidsdomain.com/kids/links/Horses.html
Links to many interesting web sites about horses

Literally Horses for Kids
donnacsmith.tripod.com/LiterallyHorsesForKids
Stories, essays, poems, artwork, and horse photos, collected by and for kids

World Almanac for Kids
www.worldalmanacforkids.com/explore/animals/horse.html
Facts, games, and helpful information about horses

Publisher's note to educators and parents: Our editors have carefully reviewed these
Web sites to ensure that they are suitable for children. Many Web sites change frequently,
however, and we cannot guarantee that a site's future contents will continue to meet our
high standards of quality and educational value. Be advised that children should be closely
supervised whenever they access the Internet.

Index